John Cena

ELBOW GREASE

FLASH

ELBOW GREASE

JOHN CENA

ELBOW GREASE

Hey, that's me!

Illustrated by Howard McWilliam

Random House 🏠 New York

Elbow Grease was the smallest truck in the Demolition Derby, but he never let that bother him.

Why should I?

His brother Tank was tougher.

His brother Flash was faster.

His brother Pinball was smarter.

His brother Crash was braver.

Okay, we get the point.

What Elbow Grease had was GUMPTION.

You got that right, Buster.

He always tried his best and never, ever gave up.

Ouch!

At night, Mel the mechanic plugged in Elbow Grease to charge while the other trucks slept outside. Sometimes his brothers teased him for being different.

Elbow Grease didn't get upset. He was glad
to be inside, especially during storms.

Then one night, Mel brought home a poster.

Someday, I'm gonna be on a poster.

The brothers laughed.

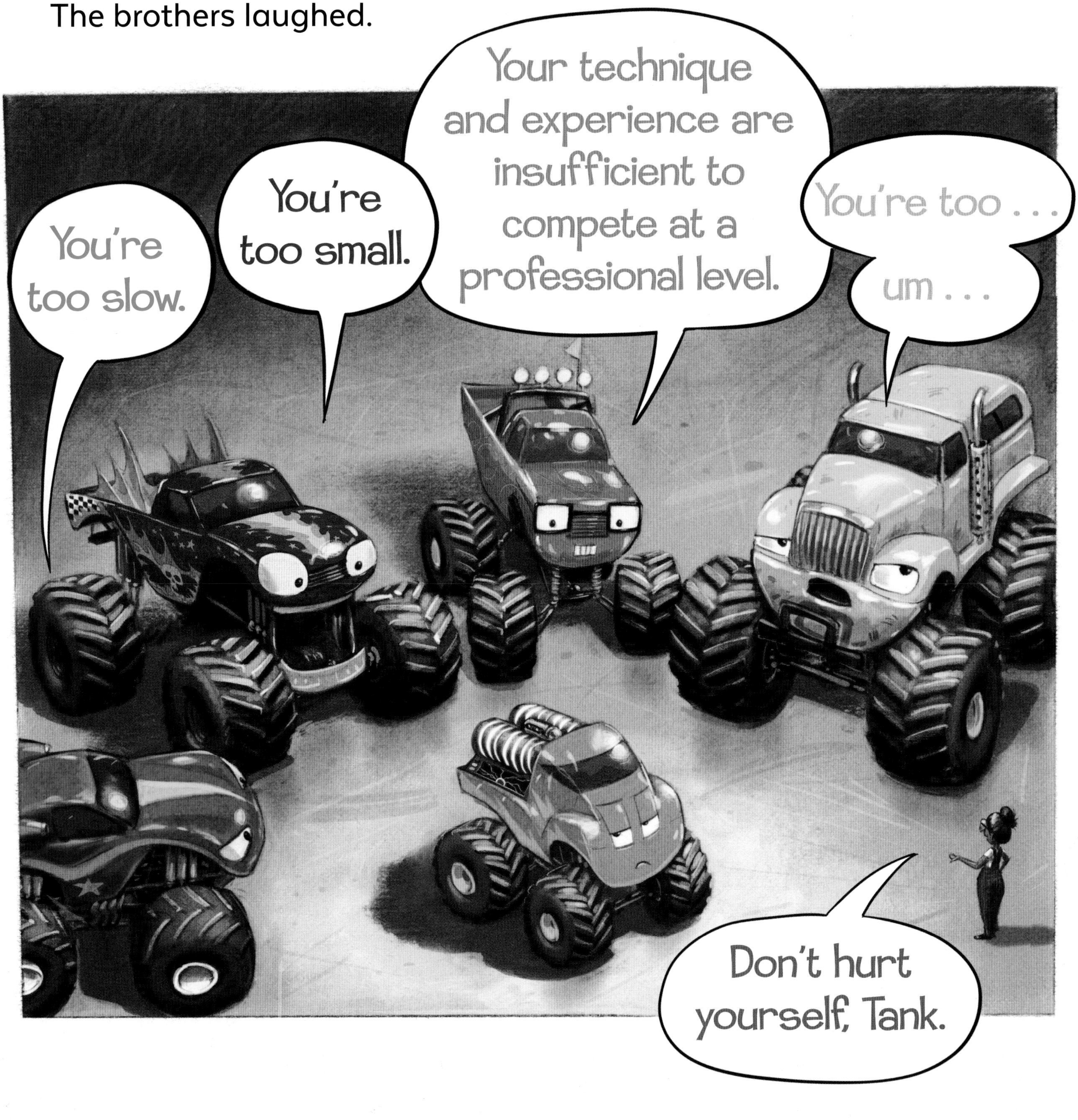

That made Elbow Grease mad! So mad that he zoomed off to the Grand Prix by himself to prove his brothers wrong.

In the morning, Elbow Grease was exhausted.
He had been driving all night without a charge.

But when he arrived at the Grand Prix, he felt his circuits surge with excitement. He quietly rolled onto the track and snuck into position behind the monster trucks at the starting line. The race was about to begin.

On your mark, get set, GO!

The other trucks were bigger. The other trucks were faster. The other trucks had more experience and better technique.

He fell behind, but he kept on trucking.

He got covered in mud, but he kept on rolling.

He got bashed and smashed and even caught on fire
a little bit, but still—HE KEPT ON GOING!

Halfway through the race, it started pouring rain.
Thunder rumbled. Lightning flashed. All of a sudden,
Elbow Grease's engine shut down. His battery was
completely dead.

The lightning jolted the battery back to life! Elbow Grease barely had enough charge to keep going, but he didn't give up. He didn't give in. No matter what, he would finish this race—even if he came in last.

Mel and Elbow Grease's brothers arrived just in time to see him rattle across the finish line and collapse in a heap. The winner's celebration was already over.

Ugh.

Mel knew that Big Wheels McGee was right.

THE END

Copyright © 2018 by John F. A. Cena Entertainment, Inc.

All rights reserved. Published in the United States by Random House Children's Books,
a division of Penguin Random House LLC, New York.

Random House and the colophon are registered trademarks of Penguin Random House LLC.

Visit us on the Web! rhcbooks.com

Educators and librarians, for a variety of teaching tools, visit us at RHTeachersLibrarians.com

Library of Congress Cataloging-in-Publication Data
Names: Cena, John, author. | McWilliam, Howard, illustrator.
Title: Elbow Grease / by John Cena ; illustrated by Howard McWilliam.
Description: New York : Random House, [2018] | Summary: Elbow Grease, a small, electric truck with a lot of gumption,
enters the Monster Truck Grand Prix to prove to his brothers that he is just as capable as they are.
Identifiers: LCCN 2017054309 (print) | LCCN 2018001487 (ebook)
ISBN 978-1-5247-7350-2 (trade) — ISBN 978-1-5247-7351-9 (lib. bdg.) — ISBN 978-1-5247-7352-6 (ebook)
Subjects: | CYAC: Monster trucks—Fiction. | Trucks—Fiction. | Determination (Personality trait)—Fiction. |
Ability—Fiction. | Brothers—Fiction.
Classification: LCC PZ7.1.C4648 (ebook) | LCC PZ7.1.C4648 Elb 2018 (print) | DDC [E]—dc23

MANUFACTURED IN CHINA
10 9 8 7 6 5 4 3 2 1
First Edition